The Adventures of the Bean People

Stephen F. Carr

AuthorHouse™ UK
1663 Liberty Drive
Bloomington, IN 47403 USA
www.authorhouse.co.uk
UK TFN: 0800 0148641 (Toll Free inside the UK)
UK Local: 02036 956322 (+44 20 3695 6322 from outside the UK)

Because of the dynamic nature of the Internet, any web addresses or links contained in this book may have changed since publication and may no longer be valid. The views expressed in this work are solely those of the author and do not necessarily reflect the views of the publisher, and the publisher hereby disclaims any responsibility for them.

Any people depicted in stock imagery provided by Getty Images are models, and such images are being used for illustrative purposes only.
Certain stock imagery © Getty Images.

This book is printed on acid-free paper.

ISBN: 978-1-6655-9719-7 (sc)
978-1-6655-9720-3 (e)

Print information available on the last page.

Published by AuthorHouse 03/02/2022

authorHOUSE®

I dedicate this book to my lovely wife, Gail, for her
help and support in getting my book published.
To my daughter Stephanie and son Richard.
My grandchildren - Sophie, Kacie, Arya, Alfie,
and baby Ray for their encouragement.

Special thanks to mum for her belief in me.

Table of Contents

Celebration Day

Pinto Bean was in town buying supplies when the mayor approached him and said "Can I have a moment with you please?"

"Sure! What can I do for you, mayor?"

"Well it's beans town's 100th year on Sunday week and we are thinking of putting on a celebration and we wondered if you had any ideas." Pinto Bean thought for a moment and said "That's 10 days away! Can I have a think about it and get back to you?"

"Yes, that's fine"

"And could you let Mexican Bean know?" the mayor added. As Pinto loaded his supplies on to the wagon, he said "The bandit was coming over to the homestead later so I will ask him if he has any ideas and I am sure we will come up with a good one."

Pinto Bean was racking his brain for an idea all the way home but nothing came to him. As he approached the stables, he could see Mexican Bean on the horizon riding towards the homestead. Pinto was unloading his supplies when Mexican Bean arrived, "Need a hand there, friend?" asked the bandit.

"Hello! I am nearly done here but you could put the pot on, I need to talk to you"

As the friends sat on the veranda, Pinto said that he had gone into town for supplies and the mayor had told him that Bean Town was 100-year-old in 10 days and wanted to celebrate the occasion and was asking for ideas.

"Do you have any?" Asked pinto. The Mexican Bean sipped his coffee and thought for a while. All of a sudden, he jumped up and said "How about a bar-b-que? Everyone likes a bar-b-que!" "That's a great idea! We could do a rodeo bar-b-que, with games and competitions, horse riding skills and rope tricks. It's a brilliant idea!" Said Pinto excitedly. "I will go to town tomorrow and let the mayor know. I'm sure it's a winner." The friends laughed and shook hands. Pinto fed the horses and Mexican Bean set off for his hideout, both thinking about the great idea they had come up with.

Next day, Pinto Bean rode to the town hall and told the mayor about their idea. "That's the best one yet!" said the mayor "I am sure the town folk will select this idea. We will have a town meeting. Let's go tell the bean folk." Soon everyone knew about the meeting that afternoon in the town square. When all the bean folk had arrived, the mayor and Pinto told them about the idea for Bean Town's day. Everybody agreed that's what they wanted and that they would all join in and do something to help. "Thank you, all" said the mayor, "We have a week to get everything ready so get together and decide who's doing what. Thank you, all"

"Where are we holding the celebration?" Asked Kidney Bean. "Well, I thought we could have a parade through the town out to the homestead for the bar-b-que and rodeo" said Pinto. "Good idea!" said the mayor. The next week was buzzing in Bean Town getting things ready.

Celebration day soon arrived and the bean folk were up early getting last minute things ready for the big celebration. There was Baked Bean, the baker, making some delicious cake, bread, and scones. Butter Bean, the dairy bean, made luscious butter, cream, and cheese. Coffee Bean, the café bean, made special coffee and cocoa. Refried bean, the farmer, made burgers and sausages. The Bean Town ladies were putting up bunting.

It was all good. Mexican Bean was at the homestead putting out hay bales for the guests to sit on. The tables were spread around for food and soft drinks and the bar-b-que was roaring. The mayor and Kidney Bean, the doctor, were loading the food, drink and bits and pieces for the games. It was around 10:00 o'clock when the mayor rang the church bell for everyone to line up for the parade which was to be led by Bugl'e Bean, the town musician.

Off they set from the South end of town up the main street in to the town square, around the Bean Town Jewel and up North run road toward the homestead. Bugl'e bean was at the Head blaring out music. The mayor was behind him with his staff of office and Kidney Bean was at the back on the food Wagon. What a grand parade it was! As they arrived, Pinto Bean welcomed them and asked them to find a seat as he wanted to tell them what the agenda for the day was.

"The agenda for today is... First, horse rides and games. Second, bar-b-que and refreshments. Third, the rodeo with Mexican Bean and myself, showing you rope tricks, lasso throwing and riding skills and finally, tea and relaxation. So enjoy yourselves and let the party begin!" Everyone clapped and cheered. Some got on horses and were led around. Some played games like hoopla and 9 skittles. Everyone was having such fun. Refried Bean was getting the food for the Bar-b-que ready and coffee bean was serving hot and cold drinks.

After a few hours of fun and games, the food was hot and ready to eat. Bugl'e bean rang his big metal triangle.

Clang! Clang! Clang!

And shouted "Grubs up, come and get it."

There were hot dogs, burgers, corn-on-cobs, bread buns and rolls and hot and cold drinks. Soon everyone was sat enjoying the food and relaxing. After an hour, there was an *Almighty Yeehaa* as Mexican Bean galloped from the east and Pinto galloping from the West towards each other. As they passed, they changed hats without slowing down. All the bean folk cheered and clapped as Pinto got his horse dancing on its back legs and Mexican bean rode in standing on two horses, waiving his hat. They did a few more horse tricks then it was rope tricks. They skipped in and out of a big lasso ring. They lassoed horses, fence posts, they even lassoed each other, lots of laughter and cheering rang out from the bean folk.

It was 5:30 when Butter bean called out "Tea time!" Butter bean had laid out his cream cakes, scones with jam or cream, and cheese sandwiches. Coffee bean served his special celebration day coffee, cocoa and milk for the little beans.

As the bean folk drank their tea, the mayor stood and said, "Three cheers for Pinto and Mexican Bean for a wonderful day. Hip Hip Hooray! Hip Hip hooray! Hip Hip hooray!" the crowd cheered with the mayor "And a special thank you to Butter Bean, coffee bean, and refried bean for the wonderful food and drink they put on." All the bean folk cheered and clapped as the heroes of the day took a bow. Pinto said he hoped that they all had enjoyed the show and he and Mexican Bean were proud to have been part of the 100-year celebration. More cheers and clapping rang out.

It was getting late and it was time to clean up and put the tables and hay bales away. Everyone helped to clear up before they left to go home. As the bean folk left the homestead, they said "What a brilliant day we had." Some said that they would be back for riding lessons.

After everyone had left, Pinto and the bandit fed and watered then stabled the horses. "What a great day." said Pinto. "Thank you for your idea and help Mexican Bean." As they sat drinking one more coffee, Mexican Bean said "It was good! Fun wasn't it?" Then the friends shook hands. Mexican bean got on his horse, said *Adios Amigo* and rode off to his hideout. Pinto got into bed thinking...

WHAT A BRILLIANT DAY!!!

Refried Bean's Missing Cows

Up at 6:00 o'clock as usual, Butter Bean was waiting for his milk delivery. As he looked out of the dairy door, he thought to himself Refried Bean is late today. Refried Bean and Haricot Bean own the farm just outside of Bean Town. Butter Bean was just about to phone the farm when a tractor came into view "Ah! here he comes at last." The tractor came to a stop and the farmer jumped down shouting "They are gone! My cows!"

"They are gone? What do you mean they are gone?"

"Well I went to call them in for milking but they were not there, so I looked around but could not find them. Just a broken fence. We have to find them." said Refried Bean. "Let's go to town and tell the mayor. He will know what to do."

When they reached the town, they woke the mayor up and told him what had happened. "Oh dear" said Has Bean (he's the mayor). "I hope it wasn't Mexican Bean, the bandit. Let's go and wake the Bean folk and have a meeting in the town hall in about 20 minutes." The mayor, Refried Bean and Butter Bean knocked on the doors and told the bean folk about the meeting in the town hall, and to come quickly in 20 minutes. When everyone had arrived, the mayor explained about Refried Bean's cows and wanted search parties to help find the cows. Of course everyone wanted to help. The mayor asked Runner Bean to run out to Mexican Bean's hideout and see if the cows are there.

"Ask him if he knows anything about them" said the mayor.

"Already on it." He said as he took off in a cloud of dust. "Everyone else will meet at the farm where we can sort out search parties. Let's go." When they had all arrived, the mayor sorted the bean folk into groups. "Broad Bean and Jumping Bean will go North. Baked Bean and Soya Bean will go East. Coffee Bean and myself will go West, the rest of you join up with the groups of your choice. Thank you!" By this time Runner Bean had reached the bandits hideout where he found him fast asleep, snoring rather loudly. "Wake up you bandit! Where are Refried Bean's cows?" Mexican Bean woke up with a jump.

"Cows? What cows?" he said the bleary eyed bandit.

"Refried Bean's Cows are missing and the mayor thinks you might know something about the cows."

As Mexican Bean yawned and pulled his boots on. He said "I had nothing to do with it, but as I am the only bandit, I get the blame. I can track animals so let's go to the farm and see if we can find them" Mexican bean got on his horse and rode to the farm. Runner Bean raced ahead to tell the mayor that the bandit was on his way and will track the cows and find them. Just as the bean folk were ready to go to searching, Runner Bean got to the farm and in a puffed out voice said "Mexican Bean is on his way to help."

It was about 5 minutes later the bandit rode into the farm yard. He got off his horse and asked what had happened. Refried Bean told him that his cows had gone and that a piece of fence was broken.

"Can you help us, please?"

"Well" said the bandit "It's not nice to be blamed for things I have not done, but I will help. Show me the broken fence" When they got to it he looked it over, got on one knee and pulled a piece of cow hair from a rusty nail and hoof prints. As he got up, he walked around the fence looking at the ground as headed towards the farm. As the bean folk followed, Refried Bean said, "This is silly. If they came this way, I would have seen them just a little further still looking at the ground, as the Bean folk got nearer to the farms milking parlour, they could hear a muffled mooing. As they looked inside the parlour, all the cows were lined up ready to be milked, "What? How?" said the farmer.

"I can answer that." said Mexican Bean. "One or more of the cows was having a good scratch on the fence and knocked it over. That's why the cow hair was there and they got out. Because they come here to be milked every day, they knew where to go and that's why the cow tracks led here and Refried Bean saw they were gone, panicked and went to Butter Bean to tell him instead of searching the farm "Well done." said the mayor "And I am sorry for thinking you had a something to do with it."

"Glad to be of help" said the Bandit.

"I feel so silly" said the farmer.

Everyone began laughing...

Silly Refried Bean

Help is at Hand

Every morning except for Sunday, Baked Bean gets up at 4:30 AM to make his bread and cakes so that they are fresh for the bean people when they get up for breakfast.

One morning, baked bean found there was no flour to make the bread. "Oh dear! What am I going to do? The bean people won't have any breakfast if I don't get some flour" Baked bean thought, "I know I'll go to see Runner Bean and ask him if he will run over to the next town and fetch some flour."

Baked Bean walked over to Runner Bean's house and knocked on the door *tap tap tap*. Runner Bean got out of bed and opened the door. "What's the matter, Baked Bean?" he asked. "Oh, Runner Bean, I haven't got any flour, I can't make any cakes or bread, could you run to the next town and get me some?" replied Baked Bean. "But of course" he said "I'll go now." So, off set Runner Bean sprinting down the main street of Bean Town and out into the country.

"Ahh" said Runner Bean to himself, "Nothing like a brisk run early in the morning." Meanwhile, Baked Bean went back to the bakery to warm his ovens. "I do hope runner bean can get some flour." All of a sudden "Arribba! Gimme zee cakes and bread" it was Mexican Bean, the bandit from the hills, outside of bean town. Baked Bean put his hands in the air and said, "I'm afraid I haven't any, I have no flour, I have asked Runner Bean to run to the next town to get me some", Mexican bean thought for a moment and then said, "I will go and wait in ambush for him when he comes back. "Oh, no!" thought Baked Bean. "That's all I need. What will the Bean People think of me letting them down like this" Baked bean sat down and put his head in his hands and sighed. By this time Runner Bean had the next town, "Good morning, Mr. Baker" said Runner Bean. The baker replied, "Good morning Runner Bean, what can I do for you?"

"I'm sorry to bother you but Baked Bean has run out of flour and can't bake any cakes or bread for the bean people's breakfast, could you let him have a bag of flour please?"

"Certainly! Here you are" said the Baker, handing over a large bag. Runner bean thanked the baker. He put the flour over his shoulder and sprinted out of the door and off toward bean town.

Mexican bean, the bandit, hid himself amongst the rocks and waited for Runner Bean and the bag of flour. Runner bean had slowed down a bit "Pheew! I didn't know bags of flour were so heavy, my legs feel like lead weights. But I must get back to baked Bean. He's relying on me." As Runner Bean ran around the bend out jumped Mexican Bean, "Hands up!" he shouted. Runner bean stopped put the bag down and put his hands in the air.

"What do you want? I have nothing of value"

"Oh yes you have. I want the flour" said Mexican Bean. "But you can't Baked Bean needs it. He has to make bread and cakes for the bean people's breakfast" said Runner bean. "Hard luck" said Mexican Bean, "It's mine now so scram. Get going."

Runner bean had to think fast, "What good is the flour to you? Can you bake? If you take it back to baked bean, I'm sure he will be very grateful and reward you. As you can see my legs are tired and I won't get back in time for breakfast" said Runner Bean. Mexican bean thought about it for a while. Runner Bean was right; the flour was no good to him as he could not bake. "Do you think baked Bean would give me some bread and cakes if I helped out?" asked Mexican Bean. "Oh yes, I'm pretty sure he would have!" exclaimed runner bean. "Alright I will take the flour into town for you." And as Mexican Bean rode off with the flour towards Bean town, runner bean thought "I do hope he makes it in time for breakfast."

Back at the bakery, Baked Bean had been pacing up and down worrying about Runner Bean meeting up with Mexican Bean. "Shall I go and wake the town elder and ask him? What I should do?" the Baker thought. The town elder was called "has bean" and he has been just about everything a bean could be. And everyone turned to him for advice when there was a problem. Just as Baked Bean was going to get "has bean," there in the door way stood Mexican Bean with the bag of flour. "I met up with Runner Bean, his legs were tired. He said that if I brought the flour to you I would get a reward."

"Yes, yes" said Baked Bean.

"I will give you some bread and cakes for your help." Mexican bean told Baked Bean, "You must promise not to tell anyone about me helping out. I am a bandit and bandits don't help anyone." so Baked Bean promised and said he would tell Runner Bean not to say anything.

As this was being decided, Runner Bean walked into the bakery, "I am so tired."

"Don't worry, you can have some bread and cakes and then go home to bed" said Baked bean.

As Runner Bean and Mexican Bean left the shop with their bread and cakes, Baked Bean thanked them very much for their help. Mexican Bean jumped on his horse and rode off to his hideout to eat his reward, and Runner Bean went home to bed. The Bean People woke up to fresh bread and cakes for breakfast, as if nothing had happened.

But we know different...

DONT WE!!

Panic Stations

Bean Town's biggest disaster was on its way. Chilli Bean, the vegetable shop owner, was also the towns weather bean, had said there was going to be a very bad thunder storm that night and a very bad storm it was too. It was around 9:30 in the morning and the Bean Folk could hear faint rumbles of thunder crash, *Bang! flash, flash*. Thunder and lightning was all around the hills outside of Bean Town. The rain was lashing down over the hills. Has Bean was ringing the town hall bell calling all the bean folk to the hall when there was a different kind of thunder. It was Mexican Bean, the bandit, galloping his horse into town as fast as he could. Has Bean said "I must talk to you right now" said the Bandit as he got off his horse. "Whatever is the matter" asked the wise old bean. "It's the storm, it's got me worried. I once heard an old Devon legend. Long ago, before Bean Town was built here, there was a very bad storm. The rain was torrential and it collected in the hills and the rivers built up and up until the water burst out and ran into one big river and washed right through this valley." Has Bean said that he had heard of a similar story. "But what can we do about it?"

"Well" said the bandit, "we have to get all the town folk together and get them to help save Bean Town."

Flash boom! flash, crash, boom.

The storm was getting worse and nearer. Eventually, all the Bean Folk had arrived at the town hall. "Quiet, please, settle down now" shouted Has Bean. Butter Bean, the Dairy Bean, asked "What's this all about?"

"If you all pipe down I will explain." The bean Folk settled down and Has Bean started.

"As you can see, Mexican Bean is here with us. He rode into town about 10 minutes ago to warn us about the dangers of rain water gathering in the hills and rivers around Bean Town." Has Bean then asked Mexican Bean "Tell them what could happen if the flood came." Mexican bean stood up and looked at the bean folk and told them of the old legend, warning them that if the water built up and burst out, it would flood the valley and the Bean Town would be washed away. The bean folk were stunned. You could hear a pin drop. "This is incredible" said Chilli Bean. "When I gave out the weather report I didn't realise it could be so serious!" Runner Bean asked, "What do you suggest we do about it?" "Well" said Has Bean, "We could build a dam at the North end of town and hope the water flows around us."

"Why don't we dig a big trench or a moat in a wish bone shape so the water flows around the town" said Kidney Bean, the Towns doctor and vet.

"That's a very good idea" said Mexican Bean, the bandit. "Anyone who has shovels or wheel barrows go get them and meet back here in about 20 minutes."

"I have got a tractor with a digger bucket on it" said Refried Bean, the farmer, "If it's any use."

"Yes, it's just the thing we need. It will save a lot of time and hand digging" said Has Bean. The bean folk went off home to get their tools. Soon they were all at the North end of town.

Refried Bean set to work digging the trench. He dug out the dirt and put some on each side of the trench. The other bean folk shovelled the earth into banks so the water wouldn't overflow out of the trench. With the operation underway, Mexican bean turned to Has Bean and told him of an old miners shack at the foot of the hills full of picks and shovels if we need them.

Fortunately, there was enough to go round.

Crash Boom! Flash.

The storm got worse, the rain got heavier. Everyone was soon soaked through but kept going to save their town. "Everyone with a wheelbarrow come over here and fill them stones then go and pack them into the sides of the trench so it will make them stronger!" called out the bandit. It was getting harder to hear each other as the thunder got louder and louder.

Crash Boom! Flash.

Has Bean called to Runner Bean, "Can you run out to the hills and see if the water is building up. "Yes, right away." He sped off at a blistering speed splashing mud everywhere. Runner bean is the fastest bean in in town and would get to the hills and back in no time at all. Has Bean looked around, it felt good to see everyone helping each other and working together as one. Refried Bean was about 500 metres from the town when he started to dig to the left around the town. Coffee bean looked up from his digging and said "This might just work to broad bean."

"I do hope so. Everyone is working so hard to save the town. It would be a shame if it all went wrong now" said the big jolly bean. With that, runner bean came racing back with not so good news.

"Has Bean, Has Bean, the water is getting higher and higher, the hill streams are starting to over flow" said the puffed out Bean. "We must work faster" said Mexican Bean.

Crash Boom! Flash.

Almost all the Bean folk heard what Runner Bean had said, and put that extra little bit into digging and getting stones. Has Bean asked Jumping Bean to go and see how far Refried Bean had got around the town and to let him know time was short. Of went Jumping Bean, bouncing and jumping towards bean town. As he neared the town, he saw the tractor coming back to dig to the right side of the town to make the wish bone trench. Refried Bean asked how things were going. "The rivers are about to over flow so time is short. How long do you think it will take you to finish the trench?"

"I should be done in about 20 minutes" said the tractor Driving Bean.

Flash, flash. The lightening was getting brighter. *Boom, boom.* The thunder was getting louder, the rain was getting heavier and the ground was getting muddier. By the time Jumping Bean got back to tell Has Bean that Refried Bean had finished one trench and had started the other. "He should be on his way by now." With that the tractor rumbled into view, Refried pulled up and told Has Bean that the trench was finished and that it was 2 metres deep with 1 metre banks on each side. "Well done, we are all but finished here too." "Here comes the flood water!" shouted could have bean, running as fast as he could past everybody.

"Everyone back into town now" shouted Has Bean, hardly able to hear himself. The bean folk ran inside the defensive bank waiting for the flood to come. Then came the loud rumbling noise of the flood water. Running from the hills into the trench. All the lady and Children Beans were in the all religion church safe from the storm and out of the rain. The Men Bean spread themselves along the trench to fill in any holes. Haricot Bean told the bean ladies and children that they had done everything they could to save the town and not to worry and that they just had to wait and see what happens next.

"Now, let's make some hot drinks and get some warm blankets for the bean men, they will be cold and wet when they come in" With kettles boiling and blankets being warmed, Haricote opened the all religions church door and looked out.

Flash. Boom! Flash. "Here they come." Harticote Bean opened the door wide to let them in. As they trudged through the door, there was the hot tea, coffee and warm blankets waiting for them. Mexican Bean got himself a hot cup of coffee, a nice warm blanket and said to Has Bean, "I'll go up in the bell tower and keep a watch on the trenches." A very bedraggled Has bean thanked him. As the bandit started to climb the stairs the whole church shook and the rumble of thousands of litres of gushing water was deafening, the Bean Folk were holding on to each other in fear.

And the children were crying and shaking. Mexican bean bounded up the last few steps, as he looked out of the tower a smile spread over his face, "It's working!!!" He hollered, "It's working. The water is going around the town, we did it, the town is going to be ok, were all safe."

"Hooray, hooray" everyone shouted and started to sing and dance.

Has bean called for calm and silence, everyone calmed down to listen. The all religions reverend said a prayer, and Has Bean told everyone that they saved their town by working together and how proud he was of them all. "I suggest that we all stay in the church tonight where it is warm and dry." They all thought that was a good idea. Has Bean told everyone to get some sleep as it was going to be another hard day cleaning up the mud in the town and filling in the trench. Eventually, all the bean folk were asleep except for Mexican Bean who kept watch over night just in case. In the morning, they all pitched in cleaning the mud that was in the town and filling in the trench. Except for Mexican Bean, they let him sleep. It was late in the afternoon when they had finished all the work. All dirty. All tired. All hungry. But they didn't care,

Their town was saved

About the Author

I wrote these adventures for my children and their children almost 35 years ago. They told me it's time to let all children enjoy the stories as they have.

Printed in the United States
by Baker & Taylor Publisher Services